MIGHTY SMALL

BY BARRY MASSEY

RoseDog Books

PITTSBURGH, PENNSYLVANIA 15238

RoseDog Books
585 Alpha Drive, Suite 103
Pittsburgh, PA 15238
Visit our website at *www.rosedogbookstore.com*

ISBN: 979-8-8892-5080-7
eISBN: 979-8-8892-5580-2

INTRODUCTION

Hello everyone, I am a retired World War II Marine sergeant with a few medals of honor. I grew up in a small town called Heavens Harbor on the West Coast in the good old USA. But let me correct myself before we get started, it wasn't just a small town. It was a very, *very* small town. Prior to the war, we were about 300 people. One small pharmacy, one small grocery store, one small butcher shop, and one mailbox in the square with a pond in the middle. The ducks loved it. The town had a lot of potential to become a beautiful city one day. It was just a mile off a river from the Pacific Ocean. The roads that led into Heavens Harbor were old dirt roads, but the harbor was its future. The perfect location for boats entering and leaving the ocean. The land was ripe for building, but like many of the other small towns in America, we knew life would not be easy. Our town was so small that we could not afford the schools, hospitals, and many other services that full-sized towns offered (we were fortunate to have a small-town doctor). The next town that had all the facilities we needed was fifteen miles away. We were grateful for the bus that picked us up every day and brought us home from school, but if you missed the bus, you were not going to school that day.

This is how America got started, a few farms, a few stores, and those who believed in its future, and what a future our town would have. Several of us Marines returned to Heavens Harbor after the war to find struggling families, but all had a passion to succeed. You might say it was a small town unto itself. Small businesses handed down from generation to generation continued a tradition that kept the town in a peaceful balance. As the rest of the country grew, so did Heavens Harbor.

My family and I owned the butcher shop in the square. As the years went by, a few more stores were added. Houses were built, some apartment buildings were added, and small businesses started to thrive. The square was still the central point and was now surrounded by several stores. The middle of the square was turned into a park with the pond. The river portion of Heavens Harbor became terribly busy. We created a port where all types of boats would come and go for both business and pleasure.

The Baby Boomer era was beginning. We knew that down the road we would have to be on our own. We could not rely on hospitals and schools fifteen miles away. I was a member of the town council, and as the town grew there were many decisions to be made. Not far from the square we built a small hospital, a small post office, and our greatest feat of all - an elementary school.

It is this elementary school that would prove the test of time. The following story reminds us of how a town can come together and overcome difficulties that would affect their lives - with the help of three little people.

1
A Beginning

The year is 1950 and I am now twenty-five years old with two children ages four and two in a little house just outside the square. It seemed like there were young children everywhere because there were. My mother and father, although getting on in years, were still able to manage the butcher store so I could be available to help in the construction of the town. As a former Marine sergeant, I knew how to lead. The people in the town were young and eager to grow and they needed a leader. I got my education through the military as so many others did during this era. We all leaned on each other to figure out how we could put this town on the map and benefit us all. We shared all the work and celebrated our accomplishments together. Trains and planes had not come our way yet, but that was one of our goals. One of the first things we felt we needed to do was update the roads leading into our town. With our businesses growing and a past that was historic, we needed to make our town accessible. We were all immigrants, and it was our parents that brought us here. We wanted to show off who we were and where we came from. We felt it was not only important to connect with our country, but also with the world. I fought in Europe during the war and had the privilege of meeting all types of people. I watched as their way of life was destroyed, but they always had hope of rebuilding. Although it was a frightening experience, we Marines knew what it would take to overcome any obstacles that got in our way.

So, back home, we built a small hospital, we built a small post office, but our biggest feat of all was the building of Heavens Harbor Elementary School. We preserved areas of our town for historic reasons, but knew the future was the elementary school. The school made us feel like we were home. No more bussing the kids fifteen miles away to a town that was unfamiliar to them and us. It was a great feeling to belong and be part of something that our community could share and call home. It was truly a beginning.

We wanted to connect with the other towns growing around us, so road construction was a priority. And when these roads were completed, we watched the trucks roll in and out with the materials that would help us build. We felt it was the beginning of the future of a town that we hoped one day would be a major city. A harbor that would one day become a major seaport.

We were creating jobs, a place where other people could call home. When the word got out that Heavens Harbor was a clean and beautiful place, people would come from all over the country. Some to visit and some to settle here. It was a young town with the potential for growth that people could envision.

2
WHAT HAPPENED?

What I am about to tell you are not going to believe. Although we were developing nicely as a town, a few of us decided to travel across the country to see what other cities looked like and get some ideas. Some big, some not so big. We were amazed at what we saw. Some buildings were so big with hardly more than a few feet between them. There were so many cars on the roads, it was almost impossible to cross the streets. There were trains above ground, trains below ground and nearby noisy airports. Although these cities were self-sufficient as I hoped ours would be one day, it just did not feel right. They seemed to be missing something important. We believed in our history, where we came from, and who we were. The big cities seemed to have lost a sense of origin. People did not know each other. You could pass someone in the street and never see them again. It might be the future, but not for everyone.

When we got back home, we discussed what we saw with our council and in town meetings. Although we had a beautiful new elementary school and plans to expand our hospital and future schools and new businesses as well, we felt the need to slow down. It was only the early 1950s, and we didn't want to lose our sense of community. We enjoyed our yearly celebrations. It was nice walking down the street saying hello to people that we knew and loved, people that we grew up with and people that we built this town with. We have always welcomed newcomers to our town, people to help us build and look to the future. They have come to work and start homes of their own. But we did not want to get too far ahead of ourselves. We enjoyed our way of life. We could see technology was advancing and, do not get me wrong, it was a good thing. It was important to remember who we were and how we got here. We could see cities expanding and gobbling up towns. Families that once lived next door to each other were now miles apart, some states apart. Through all the years Heavens Harbor had been a peaceful town, and we enjoyed prosperity within. When people came to visit our town either by the roads or the harbor, they left with a sense of pride knowing that a small town could flourish and keep its history in a country that was growing by leaps and bounds. Yes, we were a small town with a square in the middle, a park with a pond, and the ducks loved it.

3
2005
THE ELEMENTARY SCHOOL

I am turning eighty this year, I cannot believe it. My wife and I have had a good life. Unfortunately, some of my Marine buddies have passed on, but their families keep up a long-lasting tradition that has helped us survive in this fast-growing world. We still live in the same house, fixed up here and there but thankfully still standing. I have got several grandchildren, and great-grandchildren on the way. The square is still there with the pond and the ducks. We were fortunate to live in a climate that never got very cold, so the ducks had a great life as well. Most of the stores in the square are still there including our butcher shop. Up to now, we would avoid megastores and shopping malls coming into our town so our small businesses could survive. The town itself was getting old. We did our best with infrastructure and our best to help each other fix up homes and apartment buildings.

Our elementary school was still our pride and joy and is close to the town square. The school is old now and is a reminder of who we are and our accomplishments. It is three stories high and a half a block long. It is built with beautiful red bricks and large windows to open on those hot days. There was no air conditioning then and none added to this day. All the floors are made of wood, the classrooms are lined with old desks and chairs. There is an old-style cafeteria with an outdated kitchen and a gymnasium which could seat only 200 people. On one side of the school there is a playground for the older kids with a couple of basketball courts, a tennis court and a small softball field. On the other side of the school there is a playground built for the younger kids with swings, seesaws and slides. School repairs are an ongoing project and difficult to keep up with. The youngest grade in the school started with kindergarten and went up to the sixth grade. The middle school and high school were a lot newer and only a couple of miles away.

Heavens Harbor elementary school was unique. Besides being old and historic, it was the center for major events and celebrations. Graduations, holidays and special events were celebrated using the school and the square. Heavens Harbor was also known as HH. Our butcher store was titled HH butcher. The grocery store was HH groceries. The post office was the HH post office and so on. Kids who lived on the other side of the river were welcomed to go to our elementary school. They would get on the HH ferry, cross over to the HH port, and walk over to the HH elementary school, which just happened to be situated close to the river as well. And the ducks in the HH square pond, were known as the HH ducks.

At this point there were some towns around us coming together turning into one city, but nothing to concern ourselves with yet. HH was still self-sufficient, and we enjoyed our peaceful balance.

4
GRADUATION

It was a hot spring day in the year of 2005 and another graduation of sixth graders was about to take place in HH elementary school. This was a big event, bigger than New Year's, bigger than Christmas. The town always had a special place in its heart for the young ones. On this day, the gymnasium was packed. Not only were they able to seat the 200 capacity, but they added about fifty more for standing room only. In the front two rows were forty graduating sixth graders. On a small stage in the front was the principal preparing to call up each student to give them their diploma. The principal's name was Mr. Larry Haggle. Although a little bit wacky at times he was a good man who loved the children very much. He was about thirty-five years old, single, and very well liked among the townspeople. Due to the aging of the school and the outdated filing of paperwork, Mr. Haggle and his staff seemed to be overwhelmed at times. No matter when you walked into the school's office you were always greeted with a smile. Paperwork was everywhere and, at times, some confusion. You might say it was a controlled mess, but the graduation worked like clockwork. Being the biggest event of the year was never taken lightly.

There are three little people in the graduation class, three small people that in their adult life will never exceed four feet tall. They were born with body parts that inhibited the development of bones. It is known as dwarfism, but from here on out and during the remainder of the story they will be known as little people. They are special young men and will become town heroes in the distant future. The beautiful thing about HH people is that they treat everyone the same. No matter your color, race or size you were treated with respect and dignity.

As for the graduation, it was a celebration that would be remembered forever. Every year the townspeople rejoiced in their children. The night portion of the graduation moved to the square where the lights were bright and the fireworks awesome. Everyone in town contributed to the celebration even if no family members were graduating. All the stores in the square stayed open late. To this day I still remember the school's first graduating class and celebration. Watching my children and grandchildren graduate was a blessing. As part of the town Council, I was always involved.

I have been retired for the past ten years and my family still owns and runs the butcher shop. Many of the other stores in the square are still family owned. It is amazing how from generation to generation we kept this town from falling apart. Occasionally outsiders visit and enjoy our history and peacefulness. One of our prize packages was our harbor. It was close to the town and had the potential of handling big city life. It truly was the perfect gateway to the Pacific Ocean.

5
THE MOGUL

Well, the year is now 2020, I am ninety-five years old, and my memory has not failed me yet. My wife is still with me, and we are both fortunate to be doing well. We still live in our house, which has always been a repair in progress. We would not change our lives or what we have for anything in the world. Our children, our grandchildren and one day our great-grandchildren will have all graduated from HH elementary school. That is amazing. What family can boast such an accomplishment? Some of the friends we grew up with are still living here in Heavens Harbor while younger members of their families have moved on. The elementary school is still up and running and needs a lot of work. Our homes and apartment buildings are constantly being refurbished. The town square, although old and quaint, still looks beautiful. It is still the central point of all our celebrations. The park in the square has been kept up, the pond is still there, and the ducks still love it.

Most of our businesses are still here, struggling at times but getting by. The surrounding towns we shared our lives with are no longer there. The towns were getting bought up by real estate moguls, one being turned into state-of-the-art cities. The future was all around us. Our historic town and harbor with access to the sea was now at stake. Our city was in his way. He wanted the harbor and our precious land to complete his city of the future.

His name was Mr. James Hoffman, CEO and founder of one of the biggest land developments corporations in the world. He has degrees in architecture, business and marketing. He too grew up in a small town, and his dream of becoming a successful businessman is what motivated him. The problem was that the more successful he became, the more he forgot about where he came from. He was a giant in the real estate industry and one of the richest men in the world. No matter what it took, he was determined to complete his city of the future.

Looking out from any part of HH, it was not hard to see what he had already built around us. One could marvel at the skyscrapers that reached the clouds. An underground train system that moved people swiftly from district to district. No doubt it was the future and gaining access to the sea from our harbor would be his ultimate prize.

From his penthouse office in one of his skyscrapers he could see all of HH. For days he would contemplate what it would take to put our town out of business, pondering his next steps while viewing his city model. He had already offered to buy out everyone in the town, but by now I think you know how we felt. There was not enough money in the world to make us sell.

He was feeling a lot of pressure from his Board of Directors to complete the project and their patience was wearing thin. There was much investment from outside concerns, and he needed a plan. One that would end the existence of HH.

6
THE LITTLE PEOPLE

Prof. Bill Hunter was a special science teacher who had already been here a few years. He, like principal Haggle (still the principal of the school), was loved by all. A good-looking man of about thirty years old, he had graduated more than one university with high honors and was considered brilliant. Next to his science classroom was a private room. It was his own personal laboratory where he was conducting tests to find a cure for cancer. No one was allowed back there except principal Haggle who became a good friend. They say Hunter's classes were so much fun that parents would often be invited in for a session. His classroom experiments were harmless, and he had a special ability to teach the children. When it was time to eat lunch in the cafeteria, he always sat with them instead of the faculty and told scientific stories that amazed them.

Sandra Hoffman was a first-year English teacher.

She was the daughter of Mr. Hoffman. You would think there might be some conspiracy here between the two, but nothing of the kind. She was about twenty-five years old, pretty with a great personality. She, like the professor and the principal, loved the children. She knew how successful her father was and had no idea what he was planning. Sandra seemed to have a liking for the professor as they were seen many times talking and walking through the halls together. The professor seemed to like Sandra too, but most of his spare time was spent in his laboratory. He knew, as the principal did, that Mr. Hoffman wanted to destroy the town. If just one of his experiments were successful and a cure was found, this would put the town on the map forever and hopefully keep Mr. Hoffman out of HH.

Remember the three little people I told you about earlier? They never left HH. They got their diplomas from HH high school and got jobs as janitors in the elementary school. Bart Johnson, Arnold Armstrong and Steve Sanders were now in their mid-twenties and the best of friends. Hard and honest workers, they loved the children. Each one was about four feet tall. They lived in a house right outside the square, right down the street from where I grew up. Their backyard was like a big playground for the children, and they offered their time after school to have them come over while their parents were still working. They had a big dog, a mastiff named Bruno. You might say Bruno was kind of the town mascot. He was the friendliest and happiest dog I had ever seen. There was no doubt that Bruno loved the children, especially when they came over to play. But the funniest thing of all was watching the three boys walk Bruno. You see, Bruno was as big as they were, maybe a little bigger, and it took all three of them to walk him at the same time. Every day he would lead them to the town square, straight to our butcher shop, where he knew there was a bone waiting for him. The boys were well known in the town and never felt distanced from anyone because of their size. As a matter of fact, the elementary school was the perfect setting for the boys, since most of the children were no bigger than they were. Whether inside the school or outside in the playgrounds, the boys spent all their time with the children having fun when they were not working. Have you ever ridden a mop bucket on wheels? Just ask the children. I hear it is a blast.

They lived in a one-level house, and each had his own bedroom. It had a living room, kitchen and two bathrooms. One of the bathrooms was set up for guests, normal in size. Their bathroom, which was just as big, was made for them. The showerhead, sink and toilet were all lowered. Each bedroom was set up according to their personalities and attributes.

Arnold was the strongest of the three. He loved to watch professional wrestlers on TV. His room was filled with all sorts of weights, a chin-up bar and a still bicycle. He spends all his spare time working out. He is also into nutrition. He has a cabinet in his room filled with every type of vitamin you can imagine. He has stacks of strongman magazines and believes he will one day be in a nationally broadcast strongman competition.

Steve is the fastest of the three. If there is a track and field event on TV, he will be watching it. He turned his room into an obstacle course and times himself daily. He often pretends the entire house is an obstacle course, driving Arnold and Bart crazy. He has stacks of track and field magazines and believes he will one day be in the Summer Olympics.

Bart is the smartest of the three. You will find him in front of the TV when there is a good science program on. He turned his room into a library. He has shelves of books ranging from science and math to literature. He has had many a conversation with Mr. Hunter but has no knowledge of his laboratory. He is always reading the business section of the newspaper and hopes one day to be a contestant on Jeopardy.

I almost forgot to tell you about the kitchen. It is a normal-size kitchen with steps to help the boys reach things. But Bart was not happy walking up and down steps every time they needed something, especially from the higher cabinets. He built two small robots with awfully long arms. Their names were Stretch and Reach. They could be operated by either voice commands or remote control and were able to respond with robot type voices. There were many laughs with Stretch and Reach, as they were not the most graceful when it came to handling breakables. Dishes and glasses became a big expense, until they finally went all plastic.

7
THE PLAN

Homer Smith was an out of work teacher who was enjoying a million-dollar inheritance. He wanted to live the lifestyle that the city of the future offered. You could not be poor and live in Mr. Hoffman's city. He owned a beautiful house and drove an expensive car. Unfortunately, he was unable to maintain this style of living due to some poor investments. He borrowed money from Mr. Hoffman and his debt became so enormous he was unable to pay it off. At this point, you might say Mr. Hoffman owned him. The plan was to move Mr. Smith to HH. Have him get a teacher's job at the elementary school. Blend in and find out what it would take for the elementary school to fail a state health inspection. Mr. Hoffman knew that HH elementary school was the town's pride and joy. He knew the school was old and falling apart. If the school failed the inspection, the school would close, and the town would have to give in to his future plans. And what could be easier than to pay off some inspectors to condemn the school?

With Mr. Smith as his eyes and ears, Mr. Hoffman was putting a number of plans together concerning the town itself. The roads leading in and out of HH had to go through his city. Sanitation, recycling and other concerns were handled by companies surrounding HH. The only entrance that Mr. Hoffman did not control was the harbor. So, he brought in ships that would take up space in the harbor and not leave for weeks. People who wanted to visit HH could no longer come. He was strangling the roads coming in and the harbor entrance. The town's gas station at times would have shortages of gas. Supplies for businesses were delayed and the town's public services were slowed.

As for the elementary school, principal Haggle found it exceedingly difficult to keep up with the repairs. Although Bart, Steve and Arnold were doing their best, putting a Band-Aid on everything that needed to be fixed was not the answer. Homer Smith kept Mr. Hoffman in the loop. He would constantly be telling him about the needed repairs and how bad the situation had become. Mr. Hoffman, using his influence, was able to put together a team of state health inspectors that would arrive in one week and deem the school not structurally sound and therefore close it.

When principal Haggle got the word that there would be a school inspection in one week, he informed the janitors that they would need to work night and day to get the school in order. The boys knew this would be an impossible mission, but for the love of the town, the children, and of course the ducks, they would give it their best shot.

Upon finding out about the school inspection, Sandra Hoffman, unaware of his plan, went to her father to see if she could get his help. As she went up to his penthouse office she paused before going in. She could hear voices loud enough to make out what they were saying. She knew exactly who the two voices were, her father's and Homer Smith. They were discussing the inspection and looking forward to the school being condemned. She blasted into his office and confronted the two of them. She could not believe what she heard and told her father what an evil man he had become. She said you forgot where you came from, and power and greed had corrupted you. She told him not to go through with this or their relationship would be over. He just stood there, silent. She stormed out in tears fearing the worst. She ran back to the school and told the Professor and Principal Haggle what was going on. They knew they were in big trouble and could only hope for the best. Their fate rested with the janitors, those three little people who would have to perform a miracle.

8
THE FIRST NIGHT

The townspeople were afraid of what was happening. They could not believe that one person could have so much power to ruin their lives. They knew that change was inevitable, but to take away their peaceful way of living. The butcher shop that my family owned and other businesses in the town were now struggling to survive. The public works services that Mr. Hoffman owned, which included the sanitation department outside HH, were not coming into town as often to pick up the garbage. The townspeople, as they have always done, made every attempt to keep up with all the public services that were being denied. The town council had written and called their senators for help, but to no avail. They knew they were on their own.

Still, the key to keeping the town running was the elementary school. Principal Haggle and Prof. Hunter met with the boys (the janitors) Bart, Steve and Arnold to discuss repairing the elementary school prior to the inspection. They explained that they needed to start tonight, immediately. There was so much that needed to be done in such a short period of time. The townspeople were so busy trying to keep the town functioning as normally as possible. The school was in the boys' hands.

There were some items in Prof. Hunter's classroom that needed to be fixed. He told the boys not to go into the private room next to it. That it contained particularly important experiments that he had been working on and could not be disturbed. The boys understood and promised not to go in.

So that night the boys started what they knew would be an awfully long week. They brought Bruno along too, but all he wanted to do was play. Since it was nighttime, the boys decided to start working on the inside of the school where they could turn on the lights. They started by fixing and cleaning the hallways and then went from classroom to classroom. By the time they got to Prof. Hunter's classroom they were tired and decided to take a short break, but curiosity got the best of them. They said to themselves that we were here to fix everything and that would be a good excuse to go into the room they had promised not to enter. As they slowly opened the door, they were amazed at all the experimental equipment that was in there. As they walked around the room trying not to touch anything they came across a refrigerator. At this point they were thirsty and hoping there was something to drink inside. When they opened it up, they found some glasses filled with different colored liquids and thought it might be some type of punch. Well, it looked good to them and each one grabbed a glass and drank it. They left the empty glasses next to the refrigerator, left the room, found Bruno playing in the hallway and felt they had done enough for one night. When they got home, they went to bed and fell asleep.

9
MIGHTY SMALL

The boys woke up this morning knowing they had a long day ahead of them. Recently, Bart had reprogrammed Stretch and Reach not just to grab items that the boys could not reach, but also to cook and clean. If you thought grabbing dishes was funny, cooking and cleaning was hilarious. If you wanted your eggs sunny side up, not going to happen. If you wanted your bread lightly toasted, not going to happen. If you wanted the house to be cleaned, not going to happen. It's not that Stretch, and Reach didn't try, they were just a bit clumsy. Bart knew he needed to work on their programming, but not today.

As they walked Bruno to my family's butcher store as they did every morning, they started talking about how they were feeling. They did not understand the new sensations they were having. They dropped Bruno off at home and went on their way.

It was a sunny day in HH and as they walked to the school it looked like a storm had hit the town. Mr. Hoffman's plan was in full swing. As much as the boys wanted to stop and help, they knew their responsibility was to the school. But this was not just any normal walk to the school. Bart, as we know, was extremely smart. As he was walking towards the school, he noticed that the traffic lights and other electronic devices that were run by the town's computers systems were not working correctly. Not knowing anything about these systems he somehow felt he could help. When he walked into the building where the computers were, it did not take him more than a minute to read the manuals and figure out what was wrong and fix it. Bart felt more than smart, he felt like a genius. He thought to himself this could be a part of Mr. Hoffman's plan. He could not wait to get his hands on Stretch and Reach, but he had to get to the school first. He felt the need to get to the principal's office to straighten out all the financial papers and fix the filing system. It would be one of the first things the inspectors would look at. And for a moment, he thought about Jeopardy.

Steve, as we know, was extremely fast. While Bart was on his way to fix the traffic light problem, buses and cars were having difficulty navigating the streets. One of the many things that the boys enjoyed doing was walking and hanging out with the children on their way to school. This morning was different as we already know. The children were having difficulty crossing the streets with vehicles not knowing when to stop or go. From a distance Steve noticed that one of the children was about to cross the street without paying attention to oncoming traffic. He raced towards her with unbelievable speed, grabbed her just in the nick of time and took her to safety. He was not tired or even the slightest bit out of breath. He seemed to be able to move like a flash of lightning. He could not wait to get to the school. Moving tools and materials needed for repairs could be accomplished without waiting. And for a moment, he thought about the Olympics.

Now Arnold, as we know, was strong for his size. While Bart went off to fix the town's computers and Steve was out saving children in the street, Arnold witnessed a two-car crash due to the traffic light problem. He quickly looked around and there was no one to help. The driver in one of the cars was trapped. A small fire developed as the driver struggled to get out. The car door was jammed, and the wheel pushed up against the driver's chest. He screamed for help, but because of the fire people were afraid. Suddenly, the door flew open, the wheel was pushed away from the driver's chest and the driver was taken to safety. Yep, it was Arnold. He felt this adrenaline flowing through his body and could only think of saving the driver. He now realized what he needed to do when he got to the school—take care of anything that needed to be done with this new-found strength. And for a moment, he thought about the Strongman Competition.

The boys could not figure out what had happened. All they could do was talk about their heroic episodes as they hurried to the school. When they got there, they went right to work. Bart went to the principal's office and immediately started cleaning up all the paperwork. It was everywhere. He told principal Haggle and the entire office staff to go take a long lunch. The bills on principal Haggle's desk were piling up. It is not that the school was in financial turmoil, it is just that principal Haggle had no idea how to balance a checkbook. It never mattered after all these years because no one really cared until now. Bart was no longer just smart; he was now a genius. The math he needed to use was second nature. He had almost twenty years of checkbook errors to correct. He did not need a calculator or pencil and paper to put the school's finances in order. And all the paperwork that had been scattered all over the office was now in a brand-new filing system that Bart developed in a matter of minutes. The office was now immaculate. When the office staff returned, they could not believe their eyes. Principal Haggle's desk for the first time was in order. He could not wait to show Prof. Hunter what Bart had done and how he did it.

Steve and Arnold were hard at work as well. There were so many items that needed to be repaired both in and outside the school. For starters, the school's boiler was in awful shape. It was just as old as the school was and barely supplied the school with hot water and heat. The inspectors would surely close the school if the boiler were not running properly. Parts for the boiler were scarce and it was kept running with patchwork. Since the roads in and out of town were slowed by Mr. Hoffman, the boys needed a plan. HH hardware did not have the parts they needed. Steve, with his newfound lightning like speed, ran to the nearest hardware store outside HH to get the parts they needed. He was back in a flash. The boiler was big and heavy, and Steve needed to get underneath it to install some of the new parts. It was Arnold's turn. Once again, he felt the adrenaline flowing through his body, walked over to the boiler and lifted it up so Steve could put the parts in. When they finished repairing the boiler, they could not wait to show principal Haggle and Prof. Hunter what they had done and how they did it.

10
IT MAKES YOU BETTER

This was only the first day and everyone in the town heard the good work the boys were doing in the school. Later that day Prof. Hunter went into his private laboratory to do some more experiments and found the three empty glasses. He had a good idea of what those liquids could do to someone but had never tried it on humans. It was a formula he had been working on for a long time. He put two and two together and asked the boys to join him in his laboratory. He asked them if they drank what was in the glasses. The boys admitted they had and said if there was food in there, they would have eaten that too. The professor just shook his head and reminded the boys of their promise.

Nevertheless, one of the experiments that the professor was working on worked. It enhances your attributes. To what extent, the professor did not know, so he decided to run some tests on the boys. First, he gave superior mathematical and science questions to Bart who was able to answer everyone. He could read a 500-page book in a matter of minutes and remember it word for word. The professor was so amazed he could not wait to run tests on Steve and Arnold. He took them to HH high school where there was a track and weight room. To watch Steve run around the track at such an unbelievable speed was mind-boggling. To watch the amount of weight Arnold was lifting was breathtaking. Whoever thought that these three little people could possess such powers? But time was running out. They only had a few days left before the inspectors would arrive.

In the playground, the swings and seesaws desperately need to be repaired. Floors, ceilings and lighting fixtures needed to be fixed or replaced. The roof and sides of the school needed repair, as there were several leaks when it rained. But at least the boys now had some direction as Prof. Hunter, with the help of Sandra Hoffman, supervised the boys' work. It was a massive undertaking and got even worse when principal Haggle told them that the new desks and chairs that were ordered for the entire school were several days late in arriving. In fact, there were several other items that had not been delivered either. Enough was enough. Prof. Hunter knew with the powers that the janitors possessed anything was possible.

11
Becoming heros

Word got out that all the school's deliveries were in one of Mr. Hoffman's warehouses just outside HH. They had been hijacked by Mr. Hoffman's henchmen and guarded day and night. This infuriated Sandra. She went back to her father's penthouse office only to find a pre-celebration taking place. Homer Smith, some investors, and the Board of Directors were in jubilation that HH elementary school would soon be condemned. Once again, she pleaded with her father only to land on deaf ears. He told her that she should come work for him because within a few days she would be out of a job. As she walked out, she told him she would not work for him even if she was living in a cardboard box.

When she returned to the school, she found the professor with the janitors devising a plan. It included retrieving everything from the warehouse, finishing repairs and cleaning up the school and helping with the town. He had a couple of other tricks up his sleeve that only he and the boys knew about. He could not take a chance on anyone else finding out.

That night the town was quiet. The townspeople were exhausted from the work they were doing. They were two days away from the inspection. The professor had gotten a huge truck and drove to the warehouse with the boys. From a distance the boys could see Mr. Hoffman's henchmen guarding the building and were wondering how they were going to retrieve everything. Just then, the professor took out a box filled with several canisters. It was a sleeping gas that the professor had been working on and felt it was the perfect time to use it. He told the boys once the gas was released it should knock out the guards for about three hours. As they proceeded to put on gas masks, he told the boys that it was a good thing they had drunk the formula rather than opening the canisters. Once they knocked the guards out, the professor revealed the plan. Using Bart's skills, he told him to calculate how long it would take to empty the warehouse and fit everything into the truck using Steve's speed and Arnold's strength. The professor knew this would not take them long as he brought himself a chair to sit on and watched the three of them go to work. Within an hour, everything was back at the school. The new desks and chairs were now in every classroom and all the other items in their proper place. The school was looking great, and the guards were still sleeping.

The next day, the day before the inspection, the boys used their skills to help clean up the town. Everyone was exhausted as they watched with amazement. In a short time, they had gone through the entire town and restored its historic beauty. For the first time in a long time, the townspeople were smiling again. Once again, they felt the sense of belonging to a place that had always been in peaceful balance. Their hopes and prayers rested with three little people who had become the town's heroes. As for the ducks, they loved it.

That night, the professor called the boys together and asked them how they were feeling. The professor laughed when the boys explained how much easier it was walking Bruno. He did not know how long this new-found feeling would last. His hope was that it would last forever and be used toward a possible cure for cancer. But he also called them together to see if they were interested in doing one more job. It was the biggest job of all. A job that would require their skills to be at their best. The professor wanted to take the entire air conditioning system in Mr. Hoffman's office building and put it into the elementary school. It was late at night as they got ready. It only took Bart a few minutes to study the situation. He explained to Steven and Arnold step-by-step instructions as they quietly removed the air conditioning system and brought it to the school and installed it. It worked like a charm. The boys asked the professor what was next, and he replied, the inspection.

12
THE INSPECTION

The big day had arrived. The inspectors had not arrived yet. The town square was quiet as everyone had gathered around the elementary school. The school still had that old and historic look but was now in great condition. Anything that needed to be fixed was fixed. Anything that needed to be cleaned was cleaned. And anything that was out of order like principal Haggle's office was now in order. The town looked good as well since the businesses were temporarily closed before for the big event.

Principal Haggle, Sandra, the professor and the janitors, along with the schoolteachers, were waiting outside the school. No one wanted to go inside the school and touch anything. It was perfect. They felt there was no way they could fail the inspection.

Mr. Hoffman, along with Homer Smith and several investors, were waiting at the front door of the school for the inspectors to arrive. They were not standing near anyone else. Mr. Hoffman wanted to get this over with as quickly as possible. He knew with the inspectors on his payroll that the school would fail no matter what. He had never personally met them, as all their transactions were made through a third party. When they arrived, he had a big grin on his face as he opened the front door to the school. There were two of them dressed in white. Very of-ficial-looking. They didn't say much. They did a lot of writing on their clipboards as Mr. Hoffman followed them around the school. When they finished inside, they then walked around the outside. Mr. Hoffman was so excited. He could not wait for this day to come. His dream city and harbor were about to become a reality. The two inspectors had finished. They stood in front of the school for several minutes discussing what was on their clipboards. They then walked over to principal Haggle, handed him a piece of paper, shook hands and left. As principal Haggle started showing the paper to everyone, Mr. Hoffman grabbed it from him. He could not believe his eyes. It was a state in-spection certification that Heavens Harbor elementary school had passed. What happened? How could this be? As the investors walked away, he just stood there and watched as the townspeople started to celebrate. When he got back to his office he just sat there, staring at the huge model of the finished city that he had hoped for. He was also wondering why it was so hot in there. Two minutes later the police arrived and took him away. As they were leaving the police told him he should get his air conditioning fixed. And do not think Homer Smith got away either. He was caught trying to get on a bus to the airport.

13
PEACE AGAIN

Well, to this day everyone is still wondering what happened. You see, Principal Haggle knew that Mr. Hoffman, with his influence, would get the inspectors to condemn the school no matter what. But Principal Haggle knew what to do. As whacky as he was sometimes, he loved this town and knew its history. Every now and then he would come to my house, and I would tell him stories about how the town got started. He knew I was a leader and a sergeant in the Marines and came to me for help. I might be ninety-five years old, but I still had my share of influence with people in government. I once fought for my country and now I am fighting for my town. You might say they owed me. They switched out the inspectors and took care of Mr. Hoffman. I wished some of my friends could still be around to see what happened, generations later and still working together.

I sit on my front porch and can see the skyscrapers. Although the city around us can be frightening at times to look at, it is the future. With the help of my government friends, a new welcomed management now exists in the city. We have learned to coexist with them and keep our town in the peaceful balance that we have always known. HH harbor is back open for business and the elementary school once again is the center of our town. The stores around the square are doing well and the ducks in the pond are still loving it.

Larry Haggle continues to be the elementary school principal, still trying to keep his office in a controlled mess. Professor Hunter and Sandra Hoffman are still seeing each other, but Prof. Hunter's life is changed. The success that he has had with his experiments put Heavens Harbor on the map forever. As for our three little people Bart, Steve and Arnold, they are still enjoying their newfound powers. They are heroes of Heavens Harbor.